Adam and Joe are brothers.
They play in the woods near their house.

"Let's play hide and seek," said Joe.

"I'll hide..." said Adam.

'de me too," said Bear.

"Found you!" said Joe.
"I'll race you home.
Come on!"

"Find me! Find me!" yelled Bear.

"I want to go home..." cried Bear.

"Come to my home..." squeaked Mouse.
P.VENUS

"... too small..." squealed Bear.

"Come to my home..." croaked Toad.

"Toad's home is too wet for me," wailed Bear.

“Try my home...” called Squirrel.

"It's too high for me..." shivered Bear.

"Please, Bear, come to my home..." chirped Bird.

"It's too scratchy for me..." grumbled Bear.

“Then come to my home...” growled Fox.

"It's too dark and scary for me..."

"I want MY home..." sobbed Bear.

"Oh... There he is!" shouted Adam.
"Bear! I'll never leave you again!"

"Come on then..." said Joe.
"Let's go home."

"Yes! I want to go home...

to MY home!"

laughed Bear.

"This is the BEST home for me!"

Look out for other Tamarind titles:

Picture books

A Safe Place
I Don't Eat Toothpaste Anymore!
Giant Hiccups
Dave and the Tooth Fairy
ABC I Can Be
Caribbean Animals
Are We There Yet?
Boots for a Bridesmaid

Board books

Baby Noises
Baby Plays
Baby Goes
Baby Finds
Let's Have Fun
Let's Go to Playgroup
Let's Go to Bed
Let's Feed the Ducks

Published by Tamarind Ltd, 2005
PO Box 52
Northwood
Middx HA6 1UN
UK

Edited by Simona Sideri
Cover design by Sarah Hodder

ISBN 1 870516 79 6

Printed in China